The Dinner of Smells

Humaira Rashid

Illustrated by Jamie Lenman

White Wolves series consultant: Sue Ellis,
Centre for Literacy in Primary Education

This book can be used in the White Wolves Guided Reading
programme by readers who need a lot of support in Year 2

First published 2012 by
A & C Black
Bloomsbury Publishing Plc
50 Bedford Square
London
WC1B 3DP

www.acblack.com

ISBN 978-1-4081-5649-0

A CIP catalogue for this book is available from the British Library.

This book is produced using paper that is made from wood
grown in managed, sustainable forests. It is natural, renewable
and recyclable. The logging and manufacturing processes conform
to the environmental regulations of the country of origin.

Printed and bound in China by C&C Offset Printing Co.

1 3 5 7 9 10 8 6 4 2

Chapter One

It was a chilly evening. The moon hid behind the clouds. All the streets in the village were dark. Except for one…

A bright orange glow came from Mr Saeed's restaurant. Inside, everybody enjoyed the warmth.

Waiters hurried back and forth, with plates of delicious food – sizzling kebabs, steaming curries, crispy poppadoms, and spicy fish dishes!

The lovely smell from these foods drifted out of the restaurant.

It travelled through the streets...

...Around the market stalls...

…In between the houses…

…And through the window of a house that stood by itself, near the outside of the village.

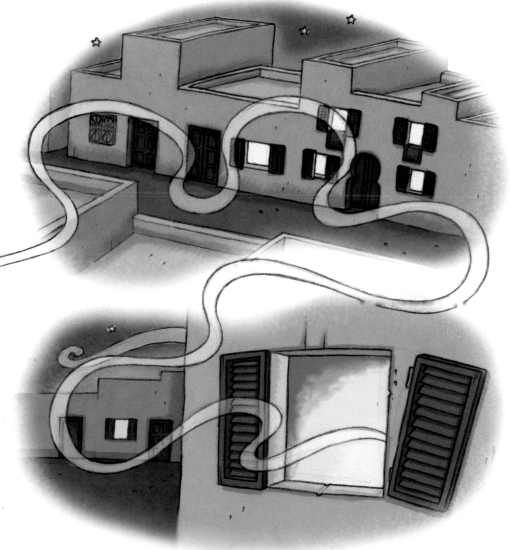

Chapter Two

In the house sat a poor old man named Ali, and his wife, Hawa.

They had no money to buy food, and were very hungry.

When the smell reached Ali's nose, his tummy rumbled.

"I will find out where that delicious smell is coming from!" he said.

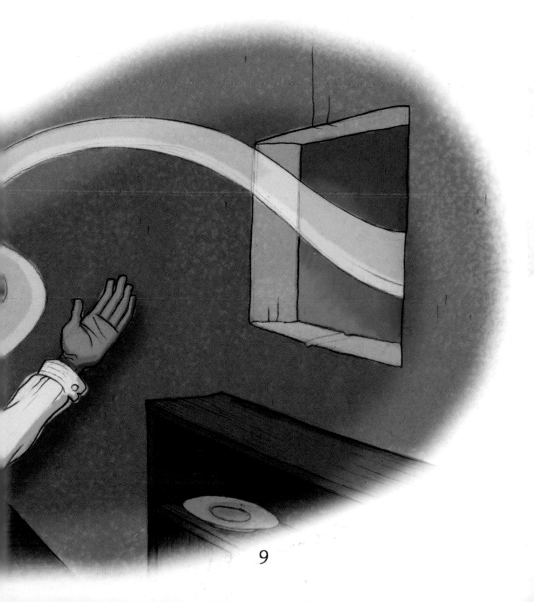

So Ali put on his old coat, and left. It was very cold, but still, he followed the smell…

…In between the houses…

…Around the market stalls…

…Across the street…

And there he saw the restaurant.

Ali was too poor to buy any food. Instead, he stood outside, enjoying the smell of the kebabs, curries, poppadoms, and spicy fish dishes.

Chapter Three

Mr Saeed, the restaurant owner, was a greedy man. He became angry when he saw Ali.

"This is my restaurant," he told Ali.
"You must pay to smell my food!"

"But I have no money to pay you!" Ali said.

"You have stolen my smell!" said Mr Saeed. "Bring me the money tomorrow, or you will go to jail."

Ali was very upset.

"How will I pay Mr Saeed?" he wondered. Sadly, with his tummy rumbling, he walked home.

Chapter Four

The next morning, Hawa had an idea. "Nasruddin will help!"

Nasruddin was a wise man, who helped many people. So Ali put on his old coat, and walked all the way to Nasruddin's house.

Nasruddin answered the door, and welcomed Ali. "You must be tired! Come in and have some food!"

Ali was thankful, but first, he told
Nasruddin about Mr Saeed.

Nasruddin sat and thought for a while.
Then, suddenly, he smiled.
"I know exactly what to do."

Chapter Five

That evening, Ali and Nasruddin came to the restaurant. Mr Saeed was waiting for them.

"Well?" he demanded. "Where's my money?"

Nasruddin held up a bag of gold coins, and shook it. The coins clinked loudly.

"Did you hear that?" asked Nasruddin.

Mr Saeed frowned. "Yes, I did."

"Well," said Nasruddin, "Ali smelt your food, and in return, you heard his money. There is your payment."

Mr Saeed turned red with embarrassment.

"Thank you for helping me!" Ali said to Nasruddin, as they walked away.

Chapter Six

The next day, as Ali was passing the restaurant, Mr Saeed stopped him.

"I'm sorry I was so selfish," he said, "I would like you, your wife, and all the poor families in the village to come and eat in my restaurant."

So that evening, Ali, Hawa, and all the other poor families went to the restaurant.

Mr Saeed served plates of sizzling kebabs, steaming curries, crispy poppadoms, and spicy fish dishes.

After that, Mr Saeed always gave some food to the poor people of the village – and Ali enjoyed the delicious smell every day!